Mrs. Popham's Library

Mrs. Popham's Library

Steven Schnur

iUniverse, Inc.

New York   Lincoln   Shanghai

Mrs. Popham's Library

iUniverse, Inc.

For information address:
iUniverse, Inc.
2021 Pine Lake Road, Suite 100
Lincoln, NE 68512
www.iuniverse.com

FIRST EDITION

ISBN: 0-595-30163-0

Printed in the United States of America

for the teachers and staff of
Greenacres Elementary School

hen Julius unlocked the library Monday morning and began emptying the waste paper baskets, he noticed thick black dust on the floor by one of the bookshelves.

"Kids," he muttered, returning to his utility closet for a dust pan and broom. "No matter how often you tell them to wipe their feet, they still track in mud."

$\mathcal{A}$

$\mathcal{B}$

C

He swept the floor below the poetry shelf, wondering how he had missed so much dirt Friday afternoon. "These old eyes just aren't what they used to be," he decided, rolling his big gray garbage barrel out the door and down the hall toward the classrooms.

Mrs. Popham, the librarian, arrived ten minutes later, her arms filled with the new books she had taken home to read over the weekend. She was feeling particularly cheerful that morning, having just finished a story over breakfast about an old woman who had taught herself to fly.

   "'I've got wings!' the old woman cried as

she soared above her walker." Repeating those words to herself, Mrs. Popham bounced into the library on her toes, feeling light enough to take flight.

S he began the day as she began every day, by inspecting the shelves, making sure all the books were neatly lined up, that those left out on tables had been reshelved, and that the newest additions were standing prominently on top of the bookcases for everyone to see.

At the History section she pushed and pulled several thick volumes into proper position. As she did so, a fine black dust drifted off the shelf onto her clean white

HISTORY

rocks

Rocks

ROCKS

shoes. She didn't notice it until she reached the science books. The shelf looked as though someone had sprinkled sand on it.

"I wish Julius would dust more often," Mrs. Popham thought, wetting a paper towel and running it across the dirty shelf. She barely had time to reshelve two biographies before the bell rang and the first students hurried into the library.

L ittle Leonard came through the door panting. He borrowed the same two books every Friday, *The Extremely Hungry Dinosaur* and *rocks, Rocks, ROCKS!*

"Morning, Mrs. Popham," he said, placing

his books on the return cart.

"Morning Leonard," Mrs. Popham
answered. "Did you have a nice weekend?"

"Sort of," he replied.

"Why only *sort of?*" she asked.

"Because somebody erased the last page of
the dinosaur book."

"*Erased it?*" Mrs. Popham repeated,
wondering if she had heard right.

"Look," he said, opening to the back. As
he did, black dust fell to the check-out desk.
And sure enough, the last page was blank. But
not only the last page, the one before it as well,

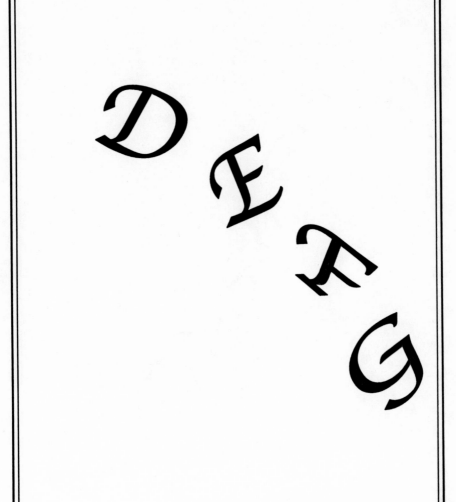

TYRANNOSAU

and half of another.

"What in the world!" Mrs. Popham muttered, running her hand over the half-empty
page. Beneath her fingers, the remaining letters
slipped off the paper and drifted slowly to the
desk, like snowflakes.

"Wow!" Leonard said. "How'd you do
that?"

"I don't know," Mrs. Popham replied, her
mouth hanging open.

The two of them looked down at the
desktop. It was covered with tiny letters,
hundreds of them. Leonard found a capital L
and an e and an n among all the commas and
quotation marks, and spelled out his name.

"There's my favorite chapter, 'Tyrannosaurus Tarts,'" he said. The letters had landed on the desk side by side.

Mrs. Popham peered through her reading glasses, then fanned the pages of the book. "Oh, my goodness!" she cried. A shower of type drifted through the air. Trembling, she slammed the book shut and set it on the desk. Then slowly, carefully, she opened to the middle. The pages were blank, except for a jumble of letters in the center, where the pages met.

Two more children arrived, then a group of six. The second bell rang and Ms. Hartwell's class trooped in, returning the books they had

13

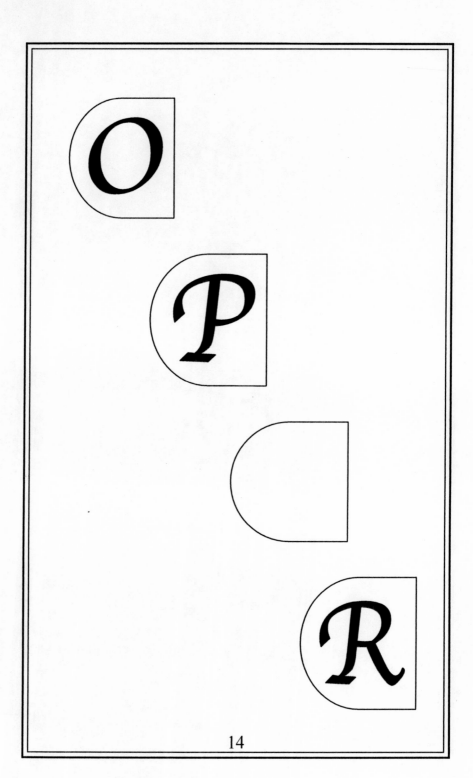

borrowed the week before. Mrs. Popham was so busy checking books in, stamping books out, and trying to keep order, that she didn't have a moment to think about what had just happened to Leonard's dinosaur book.

But when Sally with both front teeth missing, called out, "Mrs. Popham, I can't find the letter Q in the dictionary," Mrs. Popham cried, "Oh, no, not the dictionary, too!" and ran to her side.

All the children looked up in surprise. Then Mrs. Popham laughed and said, "Sally, *Q* comes after *P*, not *T*," and quickly checked to make sure all the letters were where they should be. After Ms. Hartwell's class left, she picked up the dictionary and shook it, letting all the pages flap back and forth. Nothing fell out.

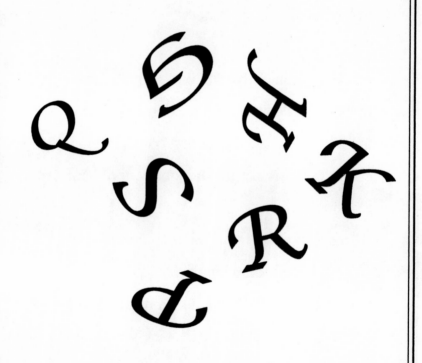

She sighed with relief.

But when she returned to her desk, Mrs. Popham found a capital *G* stuck to her thumb. "Where did *that* come from?" she murmured. Then she noticed all the letters scattered around her date stamp. There were dozens of them, large and small, simple and ornate. There was even a hand-painted *B* with flowers, butterflies, and green vines running through it. She recognized that one from the alphabet reader Sally had just checked out.

"What is happening to my books?" she wondered, shuddering. And then she remembered the dust by the History and Science

sections and went to take a closer look. It
wasn't dust at all, she realized; it was letters,
hundreds, maybe thousands of them!

With trembling hands, she removed a book
on the Civil War and watched as a stream of
type and a cannon ball spilled to the floor. Mrs.
Popham uttered a cry, dropped the book, and
ran from the library.

W ord of the loose letters quickly
spread through the school. By
mid-morning, the principal herself was standing beside the reference shelf holding a copy of
the encyclopedia and blowing gently on the
pages. Clouds of type, like puffs of smoke,
flew into the air.

Fiction

NATURE

Poetry

Science

Arithmetic

Geography

Biography

Sports

History

Regular classes were suspended so the students and teachers could help Mrs. Popham examine all the books. By lunchtime, the shelves were empty, the books heaped in piles on chairs, tables, and windowsills. In the center of the room, on the plastic tarp Julius used when raking leaves, lay a hill of letters taller than Leonard—millions of them.

"You could glue 'em back," Julius suggested to Mrs. Popham, leaning on his broom. "I've got plenty of rubber cement in the closet."

Mrs. Popham just sat with her head in her hands, muttering, "My books! My poor books!"

Then three boys from Mr. Grossman's

fifth-grade class began sprinkling letters in the girls' hair and blowing them in each other's faces.

"Stop that!" Mrs. Popham shouted, rising from her desk. "Those letters are precious."

But by that time, the fourth-grade boys had joined in and were slipping letters down each other's shirts. Rodney Bloch waited until Mrs. Popham's back was turned, then pretended to trip right into the center of the great pile. Like autumn leaves, the letters flew into the air and slowly fluttered back down, completely covering him. With a yelp of delight, a dozen other boys leapt into the pile, and suddenly there were letters in

A Y

K

C N W P
E
R F
D B
L U Q O

their hair, on their clothes—everywhere. In the midst of all the excitement, Sally had a sneezing attack and had to be taken to the nurse.

Mr. Grossman pulled Rodney to the side of the room and began scolding him. Mrs. Popham was about to suggest sending him to the principal's office when she had a sudden change of heart. Rodney, who always hated being in the library, had a big smile on his face. His cheeks were flushed; his eyes sparkled. Covered with letters, he was enjoying himself among books for the first time in his life. They all were. Mrs. Popham had never seen the children so excited.

In one corner, a group of kindergarten and first-grade children were gluing block letters back into picture books with Julius. The second and third graders were busy picking out their names in plain and fancy type, while the fourth- and fifth-grade girls were sticking letters on their cheeks and foreheads, spelling things like, "I-M-L-E" and "R-U-O-K?"

"This gives me an idea," Mrs. Popham thought, and hurried down the hall to the teachers' lunchroom.

When the three-o'clock bell rang, she handed each child a plastic sandwich bag full of letters and a blank book, and asked each of them to bring the book back at the end of the week with their own creation inside. By the next morning, more than half the students had

IMLE

RUOK

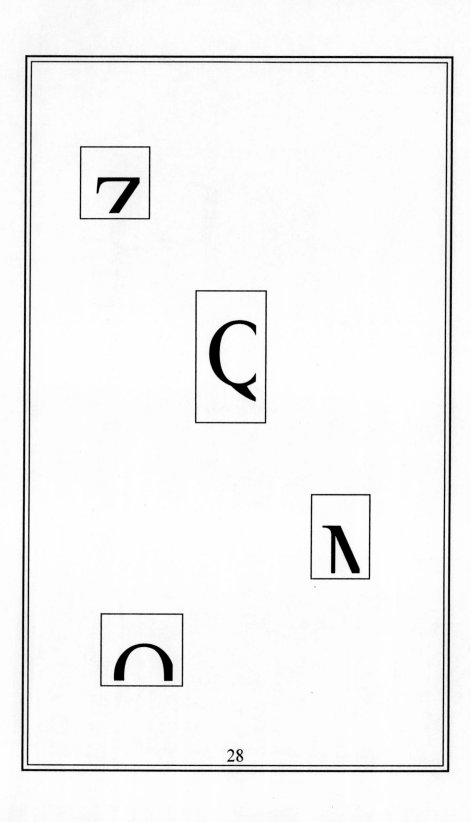

finished their books and were asking for seconds. Every book was different. Some children used the letters to write stories and poems, others to make designs.

S ally stitched letters to the page with colored thread. Leonard created dinosaurs using letters, crayons, and pebbles. And Rodney, who couldn't wait to show Mrs. Popham what he had done, had cut up and recombined the letters, inventing a whole new alphabet, complete with new names and sounds for the letters that only he could pronounce—sounds like "brrffft" and "krmk."

When the books came back, the students were just as eager as Mrs. Popham to see what their classmates had done. So, Mrs. Popham returned them all to the shelves with borrowing cards in the back and was busier than ever checking them in and out of the library.

That spring, the older children began a competition, awarding prizes for the most original design, the best story, and the craziest idea. Leonard won for his recipe book, *Cooking with Gravel*, and Rodney for writing an entire story without any vowels. Every morning, Mrs. Popham was greeted by a long line of students pushing and shoving each other, waiting restlessly for the first bell to ring so they could put their new books on display and check out the ones their friends made.

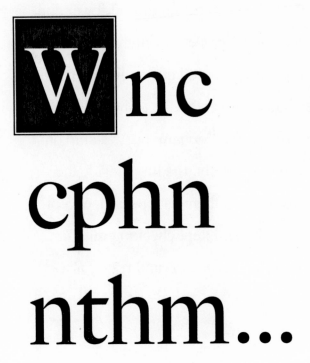

Wnc

cphn

nthm...

Summer vacation neared and Julius began to find fewer and fewer letters on the carpet. Rodney began complaining he was bored during library period and twice had to be sent to the principal's office for using Mrs. Popham's date stamp on his forehead. Gradually, the line outside the library grew shorter, then disappeared, except for Leonard, who still kept checking out *The Extremely Hungry Dinosaur* and *rocks, Rocks, ROCKS!*

On the last day of school, just before locking up, Mrs. Popham picked up a newly published book and gave it a shake, then blew on a page or two. Nothing fell out. "It's over," she murmured sadly, returning the book to the z z z z z

shelf. "But what an exciting year it was."

Glancing one last time around the library, she was about to turn off the lights when someone called her name. It sounded as though it came from the poetry shelf, but there was no one there. Mrs. Popham did notice, however, that a book of nursery rhymes had been shelved upside down. Turning it right side up, she patted it gently into place, turned off the lights, then pulled the door shut behind her as a small voice said, "Thank you."

THANK YOU

Steven Schnur has written numerous books for adults and children, including *Sanctuary, Father's Day, This Thing Called Love, The Shadow Children, Beyond Providence, The Koufax Dilemma, The Tie Man's Miracle,* and the four-volume alphabet acrostic series, *Spring, Summer, Autumn,* and *Winter*. He is a member of the writing faculty of Sarah Lawrence College and lives in Scarsdale, New York.

The Shadow Children

A terrible secret is being concealed by the residents of the French village Etienne visits every year. And this summer, odd things begin to happen around his grandfather's farm: children appear and disappear, long-lost items are suddenly found, and voices, whispering in the trees, speak of a betrayal and of a crime that the residents would rather leave buried, but the victims, and history, can never forget.

The Koufax Dilemma

Baseball is Danny's passion, but when the season opener is scheduled for the first night of Passover, he faces the same dilemma that legendary Jewish baseball pitcher, Sandy Koufax, encountered at the height of his career. How important is the game? How important is his religion? And how important is his family, divided by divorce and remarriage? Intense conflict and dramatic baseball make *The Koufax Dilemma* both exciting and thought-provoking.

Hannah And Cyclops

Everyone in Mrs. Hamilton's fifth-grade class thinks Rafi is merely clumsy, but when he keeps coming to school with serious cuts and bruises, his classmate Hannah begins to suspect that he is being physically abused by his step-father. As their friendship grows, Hannah discovers the terrible truth and tries to rescue Rafi from further harm.

The Narrowest Bar Mitzvah

When a water main bursts outside the synagogue on the eve of Alex's Bar Mitzvah, forcing a sudden and drastic change in the family's carefully planned celebration, Grandpa steps in and saves the day, helping everyone to rediscover the real significance of Bar Mitzvah.

The Return Of Morris Schumsky

On the morning of his granddaughter's wedding, the irrepressible Morris Schumsky disappears. In the midst of last-minute wedding preparations, the family is suddenly faced with the prospect that some harm has befallen Morris, unaware that he is secretly planning to make Rebecca's celebration far more meaningful than anyone had dreamed possible.

FOR YOUNG ADULTS:

Beyond Providence

Growing up on a struggling farm in the Hudson River valley, young Nathan tries to mediate the increasingly bitter rift developing between his older brother and father, a battle of wills that will eventually tear the family apart and lead to a rebirth as unexpected as it is transformative.

AND FOR ADULTS:

Sanctuary

Thirty essays, drawn from the author's columns in *The New York Times, The Christian Science Monitor,* and his hometown paper, that reflect a passionate interest in the richness and grace of daily life and the restorative power of humor.